FROM THE FILMS OF

Harry Potter

BRAVERY AND FRIENDSHIP
FILL-IN BOOK

BY **SAMANTHA SWANK**

Scholastic Inc.

ISBN 978-1-338-71599-6
10 9 8 7 6 5 4 3 2 1   21 22 23 24 25
Printed in China   68

First edition 2021
By Samantha Swank
Book design by Erin McMahon

Throughout the films, we see **Harry Potter** defeating Dark magic, standing up for what's right, and saving the day. He's one of the bravest wizards around, so it's no wonder that he was sorted into Gryffindor house at

HOGWARTS SCHOOL OF WITCHCRAFT AND WIZARDRY.

Bravery is important throughout Harry's story, but not only Gryffindors are brave. Take, for example, Luna Lovegood—a Ravenclaw through and through—who valiantly rushes into the Battle of the Department of Mysteries, and even participates in the **Battle of Hogwarts**.

What does bravery mean to you? Now's your chance to find out! This book is filled with tons of **games**, **writing prompts**, and other **activities** that will prove just how brave you really are.

TURN THE PAGE TO GET STARTED!

There are four founders of Hogwarts:
GODRIC GRYFFINDOR, SALAZAR SLYTHERIN, ROWENA RAVENCLAW, AND HELGA HUFFLEPUFF.

Each founder added a different and unique flair to the school. Have you ever wondered which founder you're most like? Answer the questions below to find out! Circle the letter according to your best answer.

The Hogwarts class you would be most interested in taking is:

A. Defense Against the Dark Arts

B. Transfiguration

C. Potions

D. Care of Magical Creatures

When you grow up, you want to be a:

A. Firefighter

B. Musician

C. Politician

D. Doctor

The best way to spend the weekend is:

A. Going on a hike

B. Reading a good book

C. Hosting a game night

D. Baking a cake

When something scares you, the first thing you do is:

A. Confront it head-on—the quicker you act, the quicker it will go away!

B. Poll your friends about the best way to tackle the situation

C. Figure out how to get someone else to do the scary thing instead

D. Pretend you aren't afraid

If the team you played for lost a game, you would:

A. Practice more for the next game

B. Figure out how many games you have to win later to make up for the loss

C. Investigate the other team to make sure they weren't cheating

D. Shake hands with the winners and say congratulations

Your friends would describe you as:

A. A leader

B. Creative

C. Competitive

D. A shoulder to lean on

ANSWERS

MOSTLY As:
GODRIC GRYFFINDOR

Godric Gryffindor was known for his bravery. His sword, the Sword of Gryffindor, helps prove it! Harry pulls the sword out of the Sorting Hat in *Harry Potter and the Chamber of Secrets* when he needs it most.

MOSTLY Bs:
ROWENA RAVENCLAW

Rowena Ravenclaw favored creativity and smarts for students in her Hogwarts house, and you likely enjoy creativity and intelligence, too! Her daughter, the Gray Lady, can be seen in the eighth film.

MOSTLY Cs:
SALAZAR SLYTHERIN

Salazar Slytherin was ambitious—a trait that many of the students in Slytherin house share. As we see in the second film, Salazar managed to place a Basilisk in a hidden chamber of Hogwarts.

MOSTLY Ds:
HELGA HUFFLEPUFF

Helga Hufflepuff founded Hufflepuff house. She was known for her kindness. Her cup was hidden by the Lestrange and Malfoy families in the seventh film.

Harry's snowy owl, **Hedwig**, was a great friend to him. The owl was a **birthday gift** from Hagrid, and she kept Harry connected to the wizarding world during his summers with the Dursleys. Using the grid, draw your own version of Hedwig below. Don't forget to include a letter for her to deliver too!

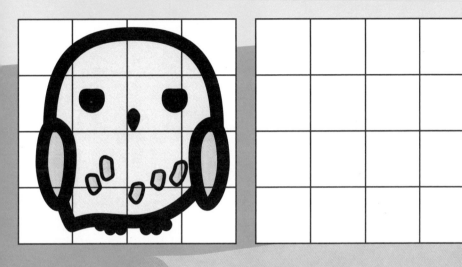

Dear Harry,

In the first film, Hermione tells Harry that there are things more important than books and cleverness—things like

FRIENDSHIP, LOYALTY, AND BRAVERY.

Who do you think is the friendliest **student** out there?
Write about them below!

_____

_____

_____

_____

_____

_____

_____

_____

Of course, friendship isn't restricted just to students! Who do you think is the friendliest **professor**?

_____

_____

_____

_____

_____

_____

_____

_____

_____

_____

_____

_____

The Daily Prophet is one of the more popular sources of news in the wizarding world. Pretend you're a reporter for *The Daily Prophet*. Then write an article about Harry below!

THE DAILY PROPHET

Will you choose his daring role in the **Battle of Hogwarts**, or perhaps how good of a friend he is? It's your article, so you get to choose! When you're done, draw in images that match your article.

WOULD YOU RATHER: GRYFFINDOR EDITION

WOULD YOU RATHER . . .

BE THE ONLY GRYFFINDOR IN YOUR FAMILY **OR** BE THE ONLY ONE IN YOUR FAMILY NOT IN GRYFFINDOR?

BE STUCK OUTSIDE THE COMMON ROOM TALKING TO THE FAT LADY **OR** ACCIDENTALLY GIVE THE COMMON ROOM PASSWORD TO SOMEONE WHO SHOULDN'T HAVE IT?

HAVE ALL OF YOUR CLASSES WITH THE SLYTHERINS, BUT NEVER HAVE TO PLAY THEM IN QUIDDITCH

OR

PLAY AGAINST SLYTHERIN IN EVERY MATCH, BUT NEVER HAVE LESSONS WITH THEM?

WIN THE HOUSE CUP IN FRONT OF ALL YOUR FRIENDS THE QUIDDITCH WORLD CUP IN FRONT OF ALL YOUR FANS?

HANG OUT IN THE COMMON ROOM BY YOURSELF BEFORE CHRISTMAS WHEN EVERYONE IS STUDYING BEFORE EXAMS?

BE THE BRAVEST PERSON IN ANY OTHER HOUSE BE THE LEAST BRAVE PERSON IN GRYFFINDOR?

BE BETTER AT POTIONS BE BETTER AT SPELLS?

EAT A BLOOD-FLAVORED LOLLIPOP EAT AN EARWAX-FLAVORED BERTIE BOTT'S EVERY FLAVOR BEAN?

HAVE DETENTION WITH PROFESSOR UMBRIDGE

OR

PROFESSOR SNAPE?

HAVE A WAND MADE FROM UNICORN HAIR A WAND MADE FROM A DRAGON HEARTSTRING?

We see nearly every character in the films do something brave—from **fighting a troll** to standing up to their friends to fending off a crowd of Dementors to **dueling Lord Voldemort**. No matter what, when it comes to proving their courage, these witches and wizards are always up to the challenge! But who do you think is the *bravest* character and why? Fill out your answers here!

I think the bravest character in the wizarding world is: _____

The bravest thing this character did was:_____

_____

_____

Another brave thing they did was: _____

_____

_____

This character is afraid of:_____

_____

_____

When this character had to face their biggest fear, this is what happened: _____

_____

_____

Now draw your character below!

FILL-IN FUN!

Which four Gryffindor students would you most want to have dinner at the Great Hall with?

1. _____
2. _____
3. _____
4. _____

Which three Gryffindor students would you most want to visit Hogsmeade with?

1. _____
2. _____
3. _____

What would your ideal Gryffindor Quidditch team be?

Seeker: _____

Chasers (there are three!): _____

_____

Keeper: _____

Beaters (there are two!): _____

_____

Who would you want to be your Gryffindor dormitory roommates?

_____

Who would you rather do a Potions class project with: Hermione or Harry? Write your answer and why below!

_____

_____

_____

If you could help the Fat Lady come up with a new Gryffindor Tower password, what would it be?

_____

Which of the Marauders (Moony, Wormtail, Padfoot, or Prongs) would you most want to sneak into the Hogwarts Library with?

_____

NOW DESIGN YOUR OWN GRYFFINDOR DORMITORY ROOM!

Be sure to draw your favorite posters, bed, and more!

What items would you want to bring? Of course, you'd need your wand, your robes, and your cauldron, but finish this list with things that you'd need for a year at the magical school—perhaps your favorite book or a photo of your best friend!

PACKING LIST

1. _____   6. _____

2. _____   7. _____

3. _____   8. _____

4. _____   9. _____

5. _____   10. _____

WOULD YOU RATHER:

WOULD YOU RATHER . . .

WORK WITH NEVILLE DURING A POTIONS LESSON **OR** WITH SEAMUS DURING A CHARMS LESSON?

HAVE TO GO TO THE YULE BALL WITH SOMEONE YOU DON'T LIKE MUCH **OR** GO TO THE YULE BALL ALONE?

PLAY WIZARD'S CHESS AGAINST RON **OR** QUIDDITCH AGAINST HARRY?

BE IN THE SAME HOGWARTS HOUSE AS YOUR BEST FRIEND AND YOUR ENEMY **OR** BE IN DIFFERENT HOUSES FROM BOTH OF THEM?

GET TO PRACTICE DEFENSIVE SPELLS WITH HARRY **OR** GET HERMIONE'S HELP ON A TOUGH ESSAY?

JOIN DUMBLEDORE'S ARMY YOUR HOUSE QUIDDITCH TEAM?

FRIENDSHIP EDITION

HAVE YOUR BEST FRIEND BECOME A PREFECT WITHOUT YOU

OR

BE A PREFECT WHEN YOUR BEST FRIEND ISN'T?

TAKE YOUR FAVORITE LESSONS WITH MALFOY, CRABBE, AND GOYLE

OR

YOUR LEAST FAVORITE LESSONS WITH HARRY, RON, AND HERMIONE?

SPEND THE WHOLE DAY IN DETENTION AFTER PULLING A PRANK WITH THE WEASLEY TWINS

OR

STUDYING IN THE LIBRARY WITH HERMIONE?

WATCH A QUIDDITCH MATCH WITH LEE JORDAN FROM THE COMMENTATOR'S BOX

OR

FROM THE STANDS WITH LUNA LOVEGOOD AND HER LION HAT?

HAVE TO DEAL WITH RON AND HERMIONE ALWAYS FIGHTING

OR

WITH CHO AND HARRY ARGUING?

In Harry's third year, **Fred** and **George Weasley** give him the **Marauder's Map**. If you had a chance to use the Marauder's Map, what would you do? Write out your adventures here—but don't forget to say, **"MISCHIEF MANAGED!"** when you're done!

_____

_____

_____

_____

_____

_____

_____

_____

_____

_____

_____

_____

_____

_____

_____

_____

_____

_____

_____

_____

_____

_____

_____

_____

_____

_____

MiSCHiEF MANAGED!

Imagine that you get to do anything you'd like for one day at Hogwarts. Circle your favorite option for each prompt below.

WHAT'S THE FiRST THiNG YOU DO WHEN YOU WAKE UP?

✶ Take your broom out for a spin

✶ Have a huge breakfast in the Great Hall

✶ Take a bath in the prefect's bathroom

✶ Head to the library to make sure you get a good table

✶ Sleep a little bit longer

WHAT'S YOUR FiRST LESSON OF THE DAY?

✶ Charms ✶ Transfiguration ✶ Care of Magical Creatures

✶ Herbology ✶ Divination ✶ Potions

✶ Defense Against the Dark Arts

WHAT ARE YOU DOiNG DURiNG THE BREAK iN YOUR LESSONS?

✶ Head down to the kitchen for a snack

✶ Get a head start on homework ✶ Go to your dormitory for a nap

✶ Talk a walk around the grounds ✶ Pull a prank

WHICH PART OF THE CASTLE ARE YOU MOST EXCITED TO EXPLORE?

✳ The Great Hall   ✳ The Astronomy Tower   ✳ The kitchen

✳ The Viaduct Courtyard   ✳ The Gryffindor common room

WHICH BOOK DO YOU CHECK OUT AT THE HOGWARTS LIBRARY?

✳ Gilderoy Lockhart's newest novel   ✳ *Advanced Potion-Making*

✳ *The Monster Book of Monsters*   ✳ *Hogwarts: A History*

✳ A book that just screams when you open it

DINNERTIME! WHAT ARE YOU HAVING FOR DESSERT?

✳ Biscuits   ✳ Pudding   ✳ Cauldron Cake   ✳ Chocolate Frogs

✳ Lemon drops   ✳ Some chocolate from Honeydukes

✳ A little bit of everything!

Have you ever wondered which Hogwarts class you'd be best at? Answer the questions below to find out which classes you'd ace!

WiNGARDiUM LEViOSA

Which bit of homework would you actually enjoy?

A. Practicing new spells

B. Uncovering secret messages

C. Doing some creative writing

D. Starting a collection

What's the best snack to have between study breaks?

A. Something I can eat in a hurry

B. Some mixed nuts—the perfect brain food!

C. A nice cup of tea

D. A veggie plate

What's your favorite outdoor activity?

A. Quidditch!

B. A brisk walk—it's good exercise and a great time to think

C. Stargazing

D. Working in the garden

What do you want to do when you grow up?

A. Something where I can protect people

B. A job where I can focus on the details

C. I'll know the right path when I see it!

D. Anything where I can work with my hands

You and your friends just saved the day! Where were you during the action?

A. Dueling front and center!

B. Working out a battle plan

C. Trying to predict what the enemy's next move would be

D. Making sure the people fighting have everything they need

How do you react when things don't go as planned?

A. Move on to plan B

B. Try to figure out what went wrong

C. Don't worry about it—everything will work out the way it's supposed to

D. Decide how you can work with what you have now

MOSTLY As:
DEFENSE AGAINST THE DARK ARTS

You'd be best at defending yourself against Dark magic. That's why you'd get straight Os—that means *Outstanding*—in Defense Against the Dark Arts.

MOSTLY Bs:
TRANSFIGURATION

Your best subject would be Transfiguration. You are determined and always focused on the task at hand—important qualities for the strong spellwork needed in this subject.

MOSTLY Cs:
DIVINATION

You are always daydreaming and thinking about the future, which means you'd excel at Divination. Plus, you're always up for a cup of tea!

MOSTLY Ds:
HERBOLOGY

Your best subject would be Herbology. You're down-to-earth and not afraid to get messy. But you also aren't wild about putting yourself in the middle of danger.

In *Harry Potter and the Order of the Phoenix*, **Professor Umbridge** assigns her Defense Against the Dark Arts students essays. Previous Defense Against the Dark Arts professors, like Professor Lupin, favored practicing spells.

What do you know about Defense Against the Dark Arts? Write an essay about it below—and hope you don't get detention!

_____

_____

_____

_____

_____

_____

_____

_____

_____

_____

_____

SPELLING TIME!

One of the most powerful tools that a witch or wizard has is their **wand**. Read each prompt below, then draw what you'd do in each scenario!

ALOHOMORA

is used to open doors. Draw the door to a room you'd really want to open!

is a spell that summons objects. If you could summon anything in the world, what would it be? Draw it below!

ACCIO

Powerful witches and wizards cast **RiDDiKULUS** to defeat Boggarts. How would you make Neville's Boggart of Professor Snape go away? Draw something funny below!

LUMOS is a spell that casts light. What's something you'd really like to see in the dark? Draw it below!

OBLIVIATE is a spell that causes memory loss. What's a memory you hope you'll never forget? Draw it here.

POTION FUN!

Of course, **potions** are important to a well-rounded magical education. Read each prompt below, then draw what you'd do in each scenario!

Veritaserum is a potion that makes the drinker tell the truth. What's something you really want to know the truth about? Why? Think about it, then write your answer and draw it below!

_____

_____

Amortentia is a special potion that smells like your favorite thing in the world. What does your Amortentia smell like?

_____

_____

_____

Felix Felicis makes the drinker lucky for a day! What would be the luckiest thing you can imagine? Draw it below!

Some of the hardest potions to brew are love potions. But wouldn't you rather have someone love you for who you are than how good your potion-brewing is? Think about who you love, then write about them below!

_____

_____

_____

_____

_____

_____

_____

_____

_____

_____

_____

_____

_____

Polyjuice Potion allows whoever drinks it to transform into someone else for one hour (like Crabbe and Goyle, or even Harry himself!). If you had a dose of this potion, who would you choose to turn into?

BEFORE

Draw a picture of yourself now on the **left** and a picture of you after you've drank Polyjuice Potion and transformed on the **right**!

AFTER

HOGWARTS WAS FOUNDED BY FOUR WITCHES AND WIZARDS:

SALAZAR SLYTHERIN

HELGA HUFFLEPUFF

GODRIC GRYFFINDOR

ROWENA RAVENCLAW

The four founders all chose something that was important to them as the foundation for their house, like **LOYALTY**, **AMBITION**, **INTELLIGENCE**, and **BRAVERY**. They were also all friends!

If you were going to create your own **wizarding school**, what qualities would you want to focus on for your own house? Who are the other founders of your house— your best friends or maybe your siblings? What qualities would their houses represent?

My house qualities are:

_____

I chose this because:

_____

The other founders of my wizarding school are:

_____

The other houses' qualities are:

_____

My wizarding school's motto is:

_____

My school's crest looks like (draw it in!):

PROFESSOR TRELAWNEY'S DIVINATION CLASSES

aren't for the faint of heart. In *Harry Potter and the Prisoner of Azkaban*, she sees the Grim—a bad luck mark—in Harry's teacup!

I SEE:

I PREDICT: _____

_____

I PREDICT:

_____

_____

_____

_____

I SEE:

Look at the teacups below. They all have some tea leaves in them. Then, on the lines underneath them, write what you see, and make a prediction for what it means!

I PREDICT:
_____
_____
_____
_____

I SEE:

I PREDICT:
_____
_____
_____
_____

I SEE:

I PREDICT:
_____
_____
_____
_____

I SEE:

WOULD YOU RATHER:

WOULD YOU RATHER . . .

DO ONE WEEK'S WORTH OF DETENTIONS WITH PROFESSOR UMBRIDGE ONE MONTH'S WORTH OF DETENTIONS WITH PROFESSOR SNAPE?

HAVE PROFESSOR TRELAWNEY FOR EVERY CLASS PROFESSOR LOCKHART FOR EVERY CLASS?

CLEAN THE CASTLE WITH MR. FILCH AND MRS. NORRIS REPOT MANDRAKES WITH PROFESSOR SPROUT?

HAVE PRIVATE LESSONS WITH HAGRID

 OR

PROFESSOR MCGONAGALL?

JOIN PROFESSOR FLITWICK'S FROG CHOIR

OR

PRACTICE QUIDDITCH WITH MADAM HOOCH?

HAVE PROFESSOR LUPIN COME BACK TO HOGWARTS TO TEACH DEFENSE AGAINST THE DARK ARTS

OR

HAVE THE REAL MAD-EYE MOODY TEACH THE CLASS?

TAKE PROFESSOR SNAPE'S DEFENSE AGAINST THE DARK ARTS CLASS

 OR

TAKE PROFESSOR SNAPE'S POTIONS CLASS?

ALL ABOUT
MAGICAL CREATURES!

What would you do before
approaching a Hippogriff?

_____

_____

_____

Boggarts take the form of what you're afraid of most.
What would be your Boggart? How would you defeat it?

_____

_____

_____

If you wanted to impress a Centaur, what would you say?

_____

_____

What's one magical creature you'd really like to meet and why?

_____

_____

What's one magical creature you'd really like to NEVER encounter? Why?

_____

_____

What would you do if you saw an injured unicorn in the Forbidden Forest?

_____

_____

What should you definitely NOT do when encountering a Basilisk?

_____

_____

What would you do if you met Aragog the Acromantula?

_____

Use these pages to write about a time you felt **afraid**. What made this moment so **scary**? How did you react when it happened? If you could use a **Time-Turner** to go back, what advice would you give yourself to feel braver?

_____

_____

_____

_____

_____

_____

_____

_____

_____

_____

_____

_____

The students in **GRYFFINDOR** are sorted into their house because of their **bravery**. But not all Gryffindors are the same! Which Gryffindor are you most like? Answer these questions to find out!

What's your favorite part about being in Gryffindor?

A. The friends

B. The respect

C. The popularity

D. A sense of belonging

E. A place to test my limits

Where can you be found in the Gryffindor common room?

A. Looking around for something I've misplaced

B. With my team, working out some strategies for the next Quidditch match

C. Telling a joke to a crowd in the middle of the room

D. Hanging out with my best friends

E. Studying by the fire

If you had to take a Muggle job, which one would it be?

A. Gardener

B. Sports coach

C. Stand-up comedian

D. Stunt person

E. School principal

What thing sounds the scariest to you?

A. Having to confront someone I disagree with

B. Being the worst at everything

C. Everyone being too serious all the time

D. Not being able to help the people I care about

E. Being unprepared for a challenge

What's the thing you're most passionate about?

A. Being myself

B. Winning

C. Making people laugh

D. Justice

E. Learning

If you weren't in Gryffindor, which house would you be in?

A. Hufflepuff

B. Gryffindor—there's no other choice

C. I would just leave Hogwarts and start my own business

D. Slytherin

E. Ravenclaw

ANSWERS

MOSTLY As: NEVILLE LONGBOTTOM

You're known for your loyalty, just like Neville Longbottom. You show bravery the most when you're sticking up for your friends.

MOSTLY Bs: OLIVER WOOD

You're competitive, like Quidditch captain Oliver Wood. Oliver led the Gryffindor team to many victories with his determination, positive energy, and passion for success.

MOSTLY Cs: THE WEASLEY TWINS

If anyone can make your friends laugh, it's you! That's why you're most like the pranksters of Gryffindor house, Fred and George Weasley!

MOSTLY Ds: HARRY POTTER

You're loyal and fearless, like Harry Potter. You're always willing to take a risk or do something dangerous if it means helping someone or saving the day.

MOSTLY Es: HERMIONE GRANGER

You're smart and determined, which makes you like Hermione Granger. You take your studies seriously, but you're also up for breaking a rule if you know you're doing what's right.

As we see throughout the films, **Dobby the house-elf** bravely risks everything to protect his firend Harry from danger. To thank him, Harry tricks Lucius Malfoy into freeing Dobby by giving him a sock. That's why Dobby loves socks so much! Design and color a pair of socks for Dobby in the space below—and remember, they don't have to match!

WOULD YOU RATHER: BATTLE EDITION

WOULD YOU RATHER . . .

DUEL AGAINST NAGINI

OR

BELLATRIX LESTRANGE?

FIGHT BESIDE DUMBLEDORE'S ARMY AT THE MINISTRY OF MAGIC

OR

BESIDE THE REST OF THE SCHOOL DURING THE BATTLE OF HOGWARTS?

HAVE TO ESCAPE THE CENTAURS IN THE FORBIDDEN FOREST

OR

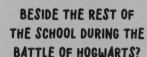

A BASILISK IN THE CHAMBER OF SECRETS?

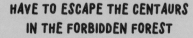

GET HIT WITH A FULL
BODY-BIND CURSE
OR
A STUNNING SPELL?

DUEL AGAINST ONE
REALLY POWERFUL
DEATH EATER
OR
THREE LESS
POWERFUL ONES?

HAVE TO FIGHT
WITHOUT A WAND
OR
WITH A BROKEN WAND?

GET ATTACKED
BY GIANTS
OR
A COLONY OF
ACROMANTULAS?

GET DUELING LESSONS FROM
PROFESSOR DUMBLEDORE
OR
PROFESSOR SNAPE?

FRED AND GEORGE WEASLEY HAVE A REPUTATION AS PRANKSTERS AT HOGWARTS.

What if Fred and George asked you to help them pull their next prank? Imagine you're at Hogwarts and complete the story below to come up with what might happen!

You're putting some finishing touches on your homework for Transfiguration in the Gryffindor common room when you see Fred and George whispering in a corner of the room. You decide to walk over and ask what they're up to. As it turns out, they are . . .

_____

_____

_____

_____

_____

_____

_____

When Harry uses the **Half-Blood Prince's** Potions book in the sixth film, he finds lots of different tricks and tips to making superior potions. Use these pages to come up with your own potion recipe!

FIRST, CIRCLE AS MANY OF THE BELOW POTION INGREDIENTS AS YOU WANT.

Wolfsbane

Wartcap powder

Unicorn hair

Essence of wormwood

Dragon blood

Gurdyroot

Beetle eyes

Snake fang

Dandelion root

Boomslang skin

Murtlap

Dittany

Porcupine quills

Venomous Tentacula

Lacewing fly

Make sure you include information about how long (and in what direction) to mix things, which order the ingredients need to be added in, and any other important steps.

My potion is called:

_____

My potion is used for:

_____

The first step to making my potion is:

_____

_____

_____

The third step is:

_____

_____

_____

The second step is:

_____

_____

_____

The last step is:

_____

_____

_____

You'll know the potion is ready when:

_____

_____

WOULD YOU RATHER:

WOULD YOU RATHER . . .

RIDE A DRAGON **OR** A HIPPOGRIFF?

KEEP GETTING SCARED BY A BOGGART **OR** HAVE TO SWIM IN THE LAKE WITH THE MERPEOPLE?

BE THE ONLY ONE WHO CAN'T SEE THESTRALS **OR** THE ONLY ONE WHO CAN?

GET SLASHED BY A HIPPOGRIFF'S CLAWS **OR** BURNED BY A DRAGON'S FIRE?

HAVE A HOUSE-ELF TO DO ALL YOUR CHORES **OR** HAVE A NIFFLER TO SNIFF OUT GOLD FOR YOU?

MAGICAL CREATURE EDITION

HELP HAGRID TEACH CARE OF MAGICAL CREATURES **OR** HELP CHARLIE WEASLEY TRAIN DRAGONS?

FIGHT A TROLL ALL BY YOURSELF **OR** BE RESPONSIBLE FOR TAKING CARE OF GRAWP?

BEFRIEND A UNICORN **OR** A PYGMY PUFF?

BRING A CAT TO HOGWARTS **OR** YOUR OWN OWL?

STORYTIME iS THE BEST TiME!

Imagine that you're at the **Hog's Head Inn**, telling a story about your valiant adventure with a **vampire** (not unlike one of **Gilderoy Lockhart's** infamous stories). What happens? What's it like? Spin your imaginary tale of bravery below.

_____

_____

_____

_____

_____

_____

_____

_____

_____

_____

_____

Godric Gryffindor left many important magical objects behind to be used by future Hogwarts students, like the **Sword of Gryffindor**. Draw a picture of what you think Godric Gryffindor looked like in the box below. Then, on the next page, draw what you'd look like holding the Sword of Gryffindor!

WOULD YOU RATHER:
BRAVERY EDITION

WOULD YOU RATHER . . .

HAVE TO SAVE YOURSELF FROM AN ATTACK BY LORD VOLDEMORT'S SNAKE, NAGINI ARAGOG, THE GIANT SPIDER?

FIGHT TOM RIDDLE'S MEMORY THE LORD VOLDEMORT ON THE BACK OF PROFESSOR QUIRRELL'S HEAD?

TRAVEL INTO THE PAST WITH A TIME-TURNER WITHOUT GETTING CAUGHT **OR** WITNESS SOMETHING IN A PENSIEVE THAT YOU CAN'T STOP FROM HAPPENING?

HAVE TO ESCAPE FROM THE MALFOYS' BASEMENT

FROM A GRINGOTTS VAULT?

PARTICIPATE IN THE TRIWIZARD TOURNAMENT **OR** PLAY QUIDDITCH WHILE DEMENTORS ARE ON THE FIELD?

BE TRANSPORTED TO THE GRAVEYARD WHEN LORD VOLDEMORT RETURNED **OR** TO THE TOWER WHEN SNAPE DUELED DUMBLEDORE?

HAVE TO PLAY YOUR WAY ACROSS A GIANT WIZARD CHESSBOARD

OR

GET THROUGH A ROOM FULL OF DEVIL'S SNARE?

THE THREE BROOMSTICKS is the perfect place to relax and swap stories! Imagine that you're at the Three Broomsticks, telling a group of travelers about your encounter with a **Hungarian Horntail**. Spin your imaginary tale of bravery below.

_____

_____

_____

_____

_____

_____

_____

_____

_____

_____

_____

_____

_____

Now write the same story—but this time, from the **dragon's perspective**!

_____

_____

_____

_____

_____

_____

_____

_____

_____

_____

_____

_____

Ocasionally, students at Hogwarts can earn an **Award for Special Services to the School**, like if they stop a monster from attacking students. The award is a way to reward students for their bravery and heroics.

What if you received one of these awards? What would you have done to deserve it?

_____

_____

Now, draw yourself receiving the award!

AWARD FOR SPECIAL
SERVICES TO THE SCHOOL

Use this page to write up an article in **The Daily Prophet** announcing the award in your honor.

THE DAILY PROPHET

_____

_____

_____

_____

_____

_____

_____

_____

_____

_____

_____

If you were in trouble against a tough enemy, what magical object would help you? Answer the questions below to discover what you would summon during your time of need.

What Hogwarts house are you in?

A. Gryffindor

B. Hufflepuff

C. Ravenclaw

D. Slytherin

How did you get into the dangerous situation you're facing?

A. You wanted to do what was right

B. Trying to rescue someone in danger

C. A miscalculation

D. Bad luck

What is your favorite thing about Hogwarts?

A. The adventure

B. Spending time with your friends

C. The lessons

D. The opportunities

What spell do you always turn to in a pinch?

A. A Stunning Spell

B. A Disarming Spell

C. An Impediment Jinx

D. A Summoning Spell

What's the first thing you would do once you've defeated your opponent?

A. Go tell everyone what happened!

B. Check on anyone else who might have been in danger

C. Figure out how to stop this from happening again

D. Celebrate!

MOSTLY As:
THE SWORD OF GRYFFINDOR

In your time of need, your bravery would summon the Sword of Gryffindor.

MOSTLY Bs:
SKELE-GRO

Woops—you likely broke something on your adventure, so this Skele-Gro would help your bones, well, regrow!

MOSTLY Cs:
A TIME-TURNER

This tool is just what you need to try the situation over again and correct your mistakes.

MOSTLY Ds:
FELIX FELICIS

This potion would ensure that every part of the situation went your way.

When Harry looked into the **Mirror of Erised** in the first film, he saw himself standing with his parents. What would *you* see if you looked inside this mirror to see your deepest desire? Draw a picture of it in the frame below.

WOULD YOU RATHER:

WOULD YOU RATHER . . .

GO ON AN UNLIMITED SHOPPING SPREE AT WEASLEYS' WIZARD WHEEZES **OR** AT ZONKO'S JOKE SHOP?

FIND YOUR WAND AT OLLIVANDERS ON THE FIRST TRY **OR** TEST OUT DOZENS OF WANDS BEFORE YOU FIND THE RIGHT ONE?

GET TO EAT WHATEVER YOU WANT FROM THE TROLLEY ON THE HOGWARTS EXPRESS **OR** GET TO CHOOSE ONE THING FROM HONEYDUKES?

STAY OVERNIGHT IN THE SHRIEKING SHACK **OR** KNOCKTURN ALLEY?

WIZARDING WORLD EDITION

HAVE A QUIET BUTTERBEER AT THE HOG'S HEAD INN **OR** A NOISY VISIT AT THE THREE BROOMSTICKS?

STUDY AT BEAUXBATONS **OR** DURMSTRANG?

GET BLOCKED FROM GOING THROUGH THE ENTRANCE AT PLATFORM NINE AND THREE-QUARTERS **OR** THE ENTRANCE TO DIAGON ALLEY?

BE THE ONLY WITCH OR WIZARD IN YOUR NEIGHBORHOOD **OR** LIVE IN A MAGICAL COMMUNITY LIKE GODRIC'S HOLLOW?

ENTER THE MINISTRY OF MAGIC THROUGH A TELEPHONE BOOTH **OR** BY FLUSHING YOURSELF DOWN A TOILET?

Every year after the first-years have been sorted and everyone has enjoyed the feast, **Professor Dumbledore** gives some important announcements and says a few (sometimes ridiculous) words.

Imagine that you are a **professor** giving the welcome speech at Hogwarts. What would you say? Think about it, then write it below! You can even make up some words, if you so choose.

_____

_____

_____

_____

_____

_____

_____

_____

_____

Being **brave** doesn't only apply when you're dueling a **Dark wizard** or protecting yourself against a **dangerous magical creature**. Any time you are scared and do something anyway, you are being brave.

What's the **bravest** thing *you've* ever done? Write about what happened here and how it felt to be brave.

_____

_____

_____

_____

_____

_____

_____

_____

_____

_____

_____

WOULD YOU RATHER:
WEASLEY FAMILY EDITION

WOULD YOU RATHER . . .

HAVE TO SHARE A
ROOM WITH PERCY

OR
WITH FRED *AND* GEORGE?

SPEND CHRISTMAS
AT THE BURROW

OR
SPEND THE
SUMMER THERE?

GET A FAMILY SWEATER
MADE BY MRS. WEASLEY
OR
A FLYING CAR THAT MR.
WEASLEY ENCHANTED?

HAVE RON AS YOUR BROTHER **GINNY AS YOUR SISTER?**

HAVE ERROL THE OWL AS YOUR ANIMAL COMPANION **SCABBERS THE RAT?**

VISIT CHARLIE IN ROMANIA ON HOLIDAY **BILL IN EGYPT?**

GET A HOWLER FROM MRS. WEASLEY **A PUKING PASTILLE FROM FRED AND GEORGE?**

In the first film, we see **Neville** valiantly defy his friends. Think about your own friend group. What's the **bravest** thing your friends have ever done? Write about it here!

_____

_____

_____

_____

_____

_____

_____

_____

_____

PETRIFICUS TOTALUS

Luna is never afraid to speak her mind. Think about a time that you believed in something others didn't understand. Then write about it here!

_____

_____

_____

_____

_____

_____

_____

_____

_____

_____

_____

_____

Quidditch is a sport that often involves an immense amount of bravery—even from the announcer! In *Harry Potter and the Sorcerer's Stone,* we see Lee Jordan bravely announce what's happening in Harry's first Quidditch match.

Now imagine that you're a **Quidditch announcer** for a game. What happens? Who wins? Write about the tale below and what you'd say!

EVEN THE MOST POLITE AND WELL-BEHAVED STUDENTS AT HOGWARTS END UP IN DETENTION *SOMETIMES.*

If you were a Hogwarts student, what would be the most likely thing to land you in **detention**? Answer these questions to find out!

What is your best quality?

A. Sense of humor

B. Ability to improvise

C. Confidence

D. Stealth

What is your worst quality?

A. Not knowing when to stop

B. Forgetfulness

C. Your temper

D. Taking too many risks

What sounds like the most fun to you?

A. Tricking a first-year into eating an entire Skiving Snackbox

B. Getting through the whole day without losing anything

C. Giving detention to your least favorite teacher

D. Meeting up with Hagrid for a late-night cup of tea

What's your greatest fear?

A. Nobody thinking you're funny

B. Getting your memory erased

C. Not being able to stand up for yourself

D. Being trapped

Which Hogwarts staff member would you *least* like to do detention with?

A. Mr. Filch

B. Professor Snape

C. Professor Umbridge

D. Professor Moody

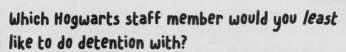

ANSWERS

MOSTLY As:
PULLING A PRANK

You're the class clown, just like the Weasley twins. And while you love making your fellow students laugh, your pranks can land you in detention.

MOSTLY Bs:
FORGETTING TO DO YOUR HOMEWORK

At Hogwarts, you would get detention after forgetting to turn in your latest class assignment. Your forgetfulness lands you in detention every time.

MOSTLY Cs:
BEING RUDE TO A TEACHER

It doesn't matter if you're snapping back with a witty retort or defending yourself or a friend, speaking your mind can have unintended consequences.

MOSTLY Ds:
GETTING CAUGHT OUT OF BED

Even an Invisibility Cloak can't keep you from detention if a teacher catches you out of bed!

Imagine that a **Howler** from Mrs. Weasley got dropped in front of the Weasley twins during breakfast. What did they do to get it? What does it say? Write about it below!

WOULD YOU RATHER:

WOULD YOU RATHER . . .

GET TO HIDE FROM EVERYONE WITH HARRY'S INVISIBILITY CLOAK **OR** SEE THROUGH ANYTHING WITH MAD-EYE MOODY'S EYE?

KNOW WHERE THE ELDER WAND IS, BUT NEVER BE ABLE TO USE IT **OR** USE THE ELDER WAND, BUT ALWAYS HAVE PEOPLE TRYING TO TAKE IT?

HAVE A FIREBOLT FOR YOURSELF **OR** NIMBUS 2000S FOR YOUR WHOLE QUIDDITCH TEAM?

TRAVEL EVERYWHERE BY KNIGHT BUS **OR** FLOO POWDER?

MAGICAL OBJECTS EDITION

BRING SOMEONE BACK WITH THE RESURRECTION STONE **OR** BE ABLE TO VISIT THEM AS A GHOST?

HAVE THE MARAUDER'S MAP **OR** HARRY'S INVISIBILITY CLOAK?

BE ABLE TO TALK TO PEOPLE IN PAINTINGS **OR** SEE EVERY PRINTED PICTURE MOVING?

BECOME AN ANIMAGUS, BUT ONLY TURN INTO A BUG **OR** NOT BE ABLE TO TURN INTO AN ANIMAL AT ALL?

GET THE SAME CHOCOLATE FROG CARD EVERY TIME **OR** ALWAYS GET A DIFFERENT ONE, BUT NEVER THE ONE YOU REALLY WANT?

HAVE A JOURNAL THAT WRITES BACK **OR** A TEXTBOOK THAT GIVES YOU ALL THE ANSWERS?

There's a big difference between a house like the Dursleys' or the Weasleys' Burrow. **Magical homes** come in much more unique shapes and sizes, and they include lots of fun quirks and features not seen in Muggle homes.

IN THE SPACE BELOW, DRAW WHAT YOUR MAGICAL HOUSE WOULD LOOK LIKE.

Is it tall and crooked? Short and stout? Brightly colored? Nothing is too bold for a wizarding home!

Now, write what kind of magical features your home would have. Get creative! And be sure to include these details in your drawing too!

_____

_____

_____

_____

_____

_____

_____

_____

_____

_____

_____

_____

One of the bravest things we see Harry do throughout the films is face **Boggarts**. Try to include everything you can remember about these magical creatures—including where they live, what they do, and how you can get rid of them.

BOGGARTS

HABITAT: _____

_____

_____

_____

_____

MAGICAL POWER: _____

_____

_____

_____

_____

Then write about it here. Don't forget to include what a **Boggart** would look like if you came across one!

APPEARANCE: _____

_____

_____

_____

_____

HOW TO DEFEAT: _____

_____

_____

_____

_____

In the images below, you'll see various **Dark creatures** and **objects** in the wizarding world. How would you **defeat** them? Would you use *Petrificus Totalus* or a Basilisk fang?

I'd defeat this by:

_____

_____

_____

_____

I'd defeat this by:

_____

_____

_____

_____

I'd defeat this by:

_____

_____

_____

_____

I'd defeat this by:

_____

_____

_____

_____

I'd defeat this by:

_____

_____

_____

_____

I'd defeat this by:

_____

_____

_____

I'd defeat this by:

_____

_____

_____

THE ORDER OF THE PHOENIX is full of some of the bravest witches and wizards around. But which member of the Order are you most like? Answer the questions below to find out!

The Order is getting ready for a battle against the Death Eaters. What do you do to prepare?

A. Make sure everyone gets a good breakfast beforehand

B. You try to gather information about the opposing side

C. You listen closely to the battle plan

D. Nothing—let's just attack!

What's your favorite thing to do when you're not dealing with official Order business?

A. Listen to some music with my family

B. None of your business

C. Meet friends at the Three Broomsticks for a butterbeer

D. Anything—as long as I can get out of the house!

Who do you think is the bravest person in the Order?

A. Everyone in the Order is equally brave!

B. Me, obviously

C. The Aurors working at the Ministry

D. The ones who were injured or captured fighting You-Know-Who

No one can agree on which battle plan is the best. Which one do you vote for?

A. The one that's the safest

B. One that I don't have to go to

C. Any of them sound good

D. You'd rather just wing it

Do you think Hogwarts students should be able to join the Order of the Phoenix?

A. Absolutely not—they're too young!

B. Of course not, they'd be useless in a fight

C. Sure, they're fun to have around!

D. Yes—anyone who wants to join should be able to

What's the worst part about the Order of the Phoenix's headquarters?

A. It's filthy!

B. The people inside

C. It's dark and cluttered

D. It's too small

ANSWERS

MOSTLY As:
MOLLY WEASLEY

You're always offering to bring snacks when you and your friends hang out. And, just like any mom of seven, you're super organized!

MOSTLY Bs:
SEVERUS SNAPE

You're brave and smart, just like Severus Snape. While your intentions are usually good, you often put your own interests ahead of others.

MOSTLY Cs:
NYMPHADORA TONKS

You're fun and a team player, like Nymphadora Tonks! You're always up for a laugh with your friends—especially if you're the one who made the joke.

MOSTLY Ds:
SIRIUS BLACK

You're a risk taker, just like Harry's godfather, Sirius Black. You're brave and always up for a challenge—especially when it comes to protecting your friends.

PROFESSOR DUMBLEDORE FOUNDED THE ORDER OF THE PHOENIX.

Using this grid, draw the esteemed headmaster!

As we see in the films, there are countless **magical jobs** to choose from, including professor, Auror, and shop-keeper! **What job would you choose**, if you got to work in the wizarding world? Write down your answers on these pages, and imagine what your life would be like!

THE WIZARDING JOB I WOULD LIKE IS:

_____

THIS JOB WOULD REQUIRE A LOT OF LESSONS I LEARNED IN THESE CLASSES:

_____

_____

_____

I WOULD LIKE THIS JOB BECAUSE:

_____

_____

_____

IN THIS JOB, I WOULD GET TO DO THINGS LIKE:

_____

_____

_____

THE BEST PART OF THiS JOB WOULD BE:

_____

_____

_____

_____

_____

THE WORST PART OF THiS JOB WOULD BE:

_____

_____

_____

_____

_____

Mrs. Weasley has a magical clock that shows where each member of her family is at all times.

Who would you include on your own clock—your family? Friends? And what sort of places would they go to? Be sure to include normal places like "school" and "home"—but also funny places like "the dentist" and "the bathroom"!

THESE PEOPLE WILL BE INCLUDED IN MY CLOCK:

_____

_____

_____

_____

_____

_____

_____

_____

_____

THE PLACES LISTED ON MY CLOCK ARE:

_____

_____

_____

_____

_____

_____

_____

_____

_____

Now that you know what to include, draw your **magical clock** in the space below. Decide where everyone is right now, and be sure to include yourself too!

Every September first at eleven o'clock sharp, the **Hogwarts Express** leaves King's Cross station from **platform nine and three-quarters**. Circle your choices for all of the below questions to show how you'd spend the **journey**.

I WOULD CHOOSE A CAR IN THE

✳ front   ✳ back   ✳ middle of the train

I WOULD SIT

✳ with my siblings   ✳ with friends from my house

✳ with friends from other houses   ✳ alone

I WOULD SPEND THE RIDE

✳ sleeping   ✳ reading   ✳ talking with friends

✳ playing games   ✳ hexing my enemies

✳ practicing spells

I WOULD GET THESE SNACKS FROM THE TROLLEY WITCH:

✳ Chocolate Frog   ✳ Pumpkin Pasty

✳ Licorice Wand   ✳ Bertie Bott's Every Flavor Beans

✳ Fizzing Whizzbees   ✳ Acid Pop   ✳ Cockroach Cluster

✳ Nothing; I brought my own

I WOULD CHANGE INTO MY ROBE

* right away   * halfway through the journey

* right before we pull into the station

WOULD YOU RATHER:

WOULD YOU RATHER . . .

HAVE HERMIONE FINISH ALL OF YOUR HOMEWORK **OR** NOT HAVE TO DO ANY HOMEWORK AT ALL?

USE A TIME-TURNER TO TAKE ALL OF YOUR EXAMS IN ONE DAY **OR** HAVE TO TAKE EXAMS EVERY DAY FOR A WHOLE WEEK?

HAVE TO DO A TON OF POTIONS HOMEWORK **OR** A TON OF DIVINATION HOMEWORK?

DO EXTRA CREDIT HOMEWORK WITH HAGRID AND HIS DANGEROUS CREATURES **OR** WITH STRICT PROFESSOR MCGONAGALL?

HOMEWORK EDITION

TAKE EXTRA HERBOLOGY CLASSES **OR** EXTRA CHARMS CLASSES?

HAVE TO WRITE A SUPER LONG HISTORY OF MAGIC ESSAY **OR** READ TEA LEAVES FOR EVERYONE IN YOUR DIVINATION CLASS?

GET HARRY TO HELP YOU WITH YOUR DEFENSE AGAINST THE DARK ARTS HOMEWORK **OR** NEVILLE TO HELP YOU WITH YOUR HERBOLOGY HOMEWORK?

HAVE LOTS OF HOMEWORK, BUT NO EXAMS **OR** HAVE HARD EXAMS FOR EACH CLASS, BUT NEVER HAVE TO DO ANY HOMEWORK?

HAVE THE HALF-BLOOD PRINCE'S POTIONS BOOK **OR** BE ABLE TO CHECK OUT ANY BOOK FROM THE RESTRICTED SECTION OF THE LIBRARY?

In the seventh film, Hermione bravely packs **EVERYTHING** the trio may need in her purse. But it's no ordinary bag—she casts an **Undetectable Extension Charm** on it! Draw a design for Hermione's bag below.

Hermione fills the bag with their **clothes, books, potion ingredients**, and **even a tent**! If you were on the run from Dark wizards and the only thing you could bring was Hermione's magical bag, what would you carry around inside? Write down your packing list on this page.

PACKING LIST

_____

_____

_____

_____

_____

_____

_____

_____

_____

_____

Harry and his friends start **Dumbledore's Army** in the fifth film to teach other students how to defend themselves and fight against **Dark wizards**.

What's something you know a lot about that you **could teach a class** on? Use this space to write about it—and don't forget to come up with a **name for your group** too!

_____

_____

_____

_____

_____

_____

_____

_____

_____

_____

DUMBLEDORE'S ARMY

_____

_____

_____

_____

_____

_____

_____

_____

_____

_____

_____

WOULD YOU RATHER:

WOULD YOU RATHER . . .

TEAM UP WITH
PROFESSOR LUPIN

OR

SIRIUS BLACK?

HAVE TO KEEP AN EYE ON
KREACHER THE HOUSE-ELF

OR

MUNDUNGUS
FLETCHER?

USE POLYJUICE POTION
TO BECOME A FAKE HARRY

OR

BE ONE OF THE GUARDS
PROTECTING HIM?

COOK DINNER FOR
EVERYONE AT
GRIMMAULD PLACE

OR

CLEAN THE ENTIRE
HEADQUARTERS
WITHOUT MAGIC?

ORDER OF THE PHOENIX EDITION

FIGHT WITH THE ORDER AT THE MINISTRY OF MAGIC **OR** AT THE BATTLE OF HOGWARTS?

BE A FIGHTER FOR THE ORDER OF THE PHOENIX **OR** BE A SPY?

JOIN THE ORDER OF THE PHOENIX **OR** DUMBLEDORE'S ARMY?

BE ABLE TO TRANSFORM YOUR APPEARANCE LIKE TONKS **OR** TURN INTO A DOG LIKE SIRIUS?

THE BATTLE OF HOGWARTS made the front page of *The Daily Prophet*! But the reporter didn't get to finish writing before the article went to press.

THE
DAiLY PROPHET

THE BATTLE OF HOGWARTS

Help them report on the story by writing your own article below. You can also draw in some images that go with the story!

IF THERE'S ONE THING HARRY POTTER IS KNOWN FOR, IT'S SAVING THE DAY!

Whether it's escaping from a dangerous magical creature or dueling a Dark wizard, Harry has survived it all. What do you think about his adventures? Write in your answers below!

Which magical creature do you think was the hardest for Harry to face? Perhaps the Basilisk, or maybe Aragog the Acromantula? Then write why!

_____

_____

_____

_____

Of the three Triwizard Tournament tasks, which one do you think was the scariest and why?

_____

_____

_____

_____

Harry's Boggart takes the shape of a Dementor. In order to defeat a Dementor, you have to think of something very happy. What is one of Harry's happiest moments?

_____

_____

What do you think was harder for Harry to battle: Lord Voldemort on the back of Professor Quirrell's head or a Boggart? And why?

_____

_____

_____

_____

Thankfully, Harry doesn't do it all alone—he's got some amazing friends to help! Do you have amazing friends like Ron and Hermione? Write about a time they helped you!

_____

_____

Some of the most exciting moments we see throughout the films are Harry's many **Quidditch matches**. Imagine you're playing Quidditch for the Gryffindor team. Then write your answers below!

MY POSITION IS:

_____

THIS IS WHERE I LIKE TO PRACTICE:

_____

MY FAVORITE QUIDDITCH MOVE IS:

_____

MY QUIDDITCH TEAM PLAYER NUMBER WOULD BE:

_____

BEFORE QUIDDITCH MATCHES, I LIKE TO EAT:

_____

Now, draw a picture of yourself in a **Quidditch uniform**! What would your Quidditch number be? Harry's is a number 7!

Ron exhibited great amounts of **bravery** in the first film, while playing **wizard's chess**. What's a game you like to play? Write about it below!

THE GAME I LIKE TO PLAY IS:

_____

_____

I LIKE TO PLAY WITH:

_____

_____

IT'S A FUN GAME BECAUSE:

_____

_____

THE RULES OF THE GAME ARE:

_____

_____

_____

Now imagine that you can **make up your own game**! What would it be like? Would it have any magic? Write about it below!

_____

_____

_____

_____

_____

_____

_____

_____

_____

_____

_____

_____

If you could learn **any spell**, which do you think would be the most useful? Fill out this bracket to find out! Then write about why below.

Alohomora   Accio   Lumos   Nox   Avada Kedavra   Crucio   Expelliarmus   Riddikulus

THE WINNER!

Confundo   Obliviate   Stupefy   Reducto   Expecto Patronum   Diffindo   Engorgio   Episkey

Harry, Ron, and Hermione are three of the wizarding world's **best friends**. They are always there for each other. Use the grids below to draw the trio!

DRAWING TIME!

Severus Snape ended up being one of the bravest men that Harry ever knew. Using the grid below, draw the **infamous Potions Master!**

Think about the friends in your life. Now write in who you think best applies to each category!

THE PERSON I CAN COUNT ON FOR ANYTHING IS:

_____

WHEN I'M FEELING DOWN, THIS PERSON
CAN ALWAYS CHEER ME UP:

_____

I WOULD ALWAYS STICK UP FOR:

_____

THE PERSON WHO BEST TAKES CARE OF ME IS:

_____

IF I HAD A MILLION TACOS, I'D SHARE THEM WITH:

_____

I LOOK UP TO:

_____

SOMEONE WHO LOOKS UP TO ME IS:

_____

WOULD YOU RATHER:
TRIWIZARD TOURNAMENT EDITION

WOULD YOU RATHER . . .

BE THE HOGWARTS CHAMPION **OR** DUEL AGAINST PROFESSOR DUMBLEDORE?

FACE A DRAGON WITHOUT YOUR WAND

 OR

FACE THE MERPEOPLE WITHOUT A WAY TO BREATHE UNDERWATER?

SCORE THE LOWEST IN THE FIRST TASK **OR** SCORE THE LOWEST IN THE THIRD TASK?

DANCE IN FRONT OF EVERYONE AT THE YULE BALL **OR** SING IN FRONT OF EVERYONE AT THE YULE BALL?

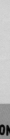

WIN THE QUIDDITCH WORLD CUP  THE TRIWIZARD TOURNAMENT?

BECOME BEST FRIENDS WITH SOMEONE FROM DURMSTRANG **OR** FROM BEAUXBATONS?

BE INTERVIEWED BY RITA SKEETER TRANSFIGURE YOURSELF INTO A BEETLE FOR AN HOUR?

FIND OUT YOUR FAVORITE PROFESSOR WAS TAKING POLYJUICE POTION FIND OUT YOUR LEAST FAVORITE PROFESSOR WAS TAKING POLYJUICE POTION?

FIGHT A GRINDYLOW FIGHT A BLAST-ENDED SKREWT?

LOSE THE TRIWIZARD TOURNAMENT, BUT BE ADORED WIN THE TRIWIZARD TOURNAMENT, BUT BE HATED?

THAT'S IT, YOU'VE MADE IT!

Sign your name here and be on your way . . . You're a true master of the Harry Potter films!

CERTIFICATE
OF
BRAVERY
AND
FRIENDSHIP
PRESENTED TO

_____

_____